OLIVIA ™
and Grandma's Visit

adapted by Cordelia Evans
based on the screenplay written by Eryk Casemiro and Kate Boutillier
illustrated by Shane L. Johnson

Simon Spotlight
New York   London   Toronto   Sydney   New Delhi

D1119028

Based on the TV series OLIVIA™ as seen on Nickelodeon™

SIMON SPOTLIGHT
An imprint of Simon & Schuster Children's Publishing Division
1230 Avenue of the Americas, New York, New York 10020
OLIVIA™ Ian Falconer Ink Unlimited, Inc. and © 2013 Ian Falconer and Classic Media, LLC
All rights reserved, including the right of reproduction in whole or in part in any form.
SIMON SPOTLIGHT and colophon are registered trademarks of Simon & Schuster, Inc.
For information about special discounts for bulk purchases,
please contact Simon & Schuster Special Sales at 1-866-506-1949 or business@simonandschuster.com.
Manufactured in the United States of America 0413 LAK
First Edition 1 2 3 4 5 6 7 8 9 10
ISBN 978-1-4424-4586-4
ISBN 978-1-4424-4587-1 (eBook)

Julian looked around Olivia's room and frowned a little bit.
"Won't you get into trouble for wallpapering your room?" he
asked.
"Oh no," Olivia replied as she carefully applied more glue to the
back of the paper. "My mom said she wanted to make the house
look nice for my grandma's visit. And since Grandma *loves*
flowers, I thought, why not put them on the wall?"

"What's going on here, Olivia?" Mother asked.

"I'm making my room pretty for Grandma!" Olivia explained.
"I have some wallpaper left over—want me to do your room too?"

"Maybe some other time," Mother said. "For now, please start
moving your things into Ian's room."

"Why?" asked Olivia. "I'm staying here in my room with Grandma."

"No, Grandma will stay here by herself, and you'll get to stay in
Ian's room. Won't that be fun?" said Mother.

Olivia wrinkled her nose as she checked out Ian's room.
"Something smells in here!" she declared. She sprayed perfume as
Julian dragged her trunk into the room.
"Mom!" Ian yelled. "Olivia is taking over my room!"
Mother came to the door. "Olivia, Ian is sharing his room with you,
but that doesn't mean you can turn it into your room," she said.

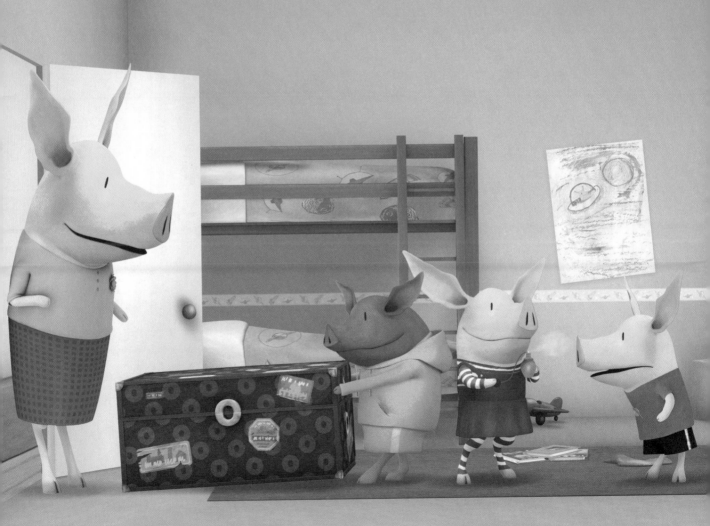

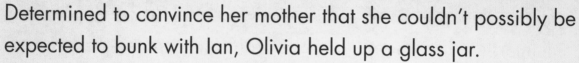

Determined to convince her mother that she couldn't possibly be
expected to bunk with Ian, Olivia held up a glass jar.

"Look, Mom, Ian has fleas! There's no way I can stay in a room
with fleas."

"I don't see any fleas, Olivia," Mother said. "Nice try. What
happened to the blackberry jam that was in this jar?"

"It was empty when I found it," Olivia said.

Later that day Olivia was trying to set up her arts-and-crafts station, but she was having trouble because Ian was zooming around her in circles on his tricycle.

"Excuse me!" said Olivia.

"Vroom, vroom!" said Ian.

Olivia wished there was some way she could escape from Ian's room. . . .

"I cannot stay locked up in this castle with my brother for another minute." Olivia sighed. "I must find a secret passage!"

"Whoa, check out the spiders," Ian said as he peered into the passageway Olivia had discovered.

"I think I'll find another way out," said Olivia.

"Olivia! Ian! Grandma's here!" called Mother from downstairs.
Olivia and Ian raced out of the room.
Grandma gathered Ian into a big hug. "I just can't get enough of
my little Ian. And where's my Olivia?"

"Here I am, Grandma!" Olivia called. She was wearing her new hat and scarf.
"Now that's style, darling!" Grandma said.

After a delicious spaghetti dinner, it was time to dance! Grandma turned on some lively music. "Listen to the beat and move those little feet," she instructed as she showed off some of her latest dance moves.

"Wonderful, Ian—you're making it your own!" exclaimed
Grandma. "That's it, Olivia! You are a natural."

Later, Olivia walked into her room while Grandma was getting ready for bed.

"I love the new wallpaper," Grandma told her.

"Thank you," said Olivia.

"Did you need something?" asked Grandma.

"I forgot my, um, ear ribbons."

Grandma looked at her. "What about the ribbons you're wearing?"

"Oh right," said Olivia, backing slowly out of the room. "Okay. Good night, Grandma."

"Good night, Olivia."

A moment later Olivia poked her head back into her room.
"Yes, Olivia?" said Grandma.
"I just remembered: I forgot my favorite slippers!" replied Olivia.
"You know, I might be a little lonely all by myself in here," said
Grandma. "Do you think you could bunk in here with me?"

"Really?" exclaimed Olivia. "You wouldn't mind?"
"I'd be delighted," said Grandma. "And I know just the thing to make this sleepover extra special! Why don't you get cozy in bed? I'll be right back."

"One sundae, two spoons," Grandma said a few minutes later.
"You're the best grandma in the whole entire world!" Olivia said as
she reached for a spoon.
"I've always said you had good taste!" Grandma replied.

"Do you always have ice cream before you go to sleep?" Olivia asked.

"Only on special occasions," Grandma explained. "Usually I end my day by thinking back to my favorite parts. Why don't you try?"

Olivia thought for a minute. "Well, I liked the pancakes I made for breakfast. And I liked it when William threw his cereal. But I think my favorite part of today is . . . this!"

"This ice-cream sundae?" asked Grandma.

"No, being with you!" said Olivia.

In the middle of the night Olivia was woken up by a loud noise—Grandma was snoring!
She tried to ignore it, but she couldn't fall back asleep. She reached over and carefully moved Grandma's head. Grandma stopped snoring.
Olivia smiled and closed her eyes. Then she heard it again.
Zzzzzzz.

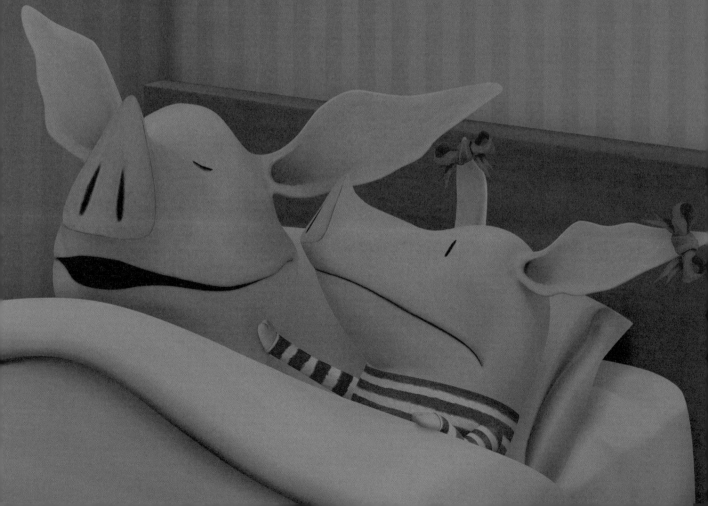

So Olivia tried plugging her ears.

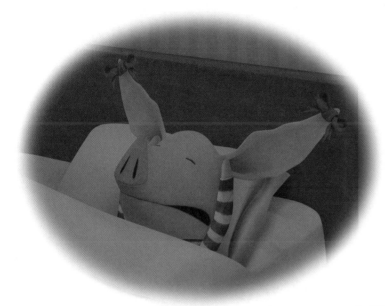

Then she tried listening to music.

But she could still hear Grandma's snores!

Finally, Olivia couldn't take it anymore. She slipped out of bed, crept down the hall, and climbed into the top bunk of Ian's bed, where she fell asleep immediately.

The next morning Olivia returned to her room just as Grandma was beginning her tai chi routine.

"I wondered where you'd got off to, darling!" said Grandma.

"I slept in Ian's room," Olivia explained.

"You did?" asked Grandma. "Why?"

"Ian was sad I wasn't sleeping in his room. But please don't tell him that I told you," Olivia said.

"I wouldn't dream of it," replied Grandma. "Besides, you know, you talk in your sleep. I couldn't sleep a wink!"

That night, Grandma read Olivia a story in Ian's room.
"What was your favorite part of today, Grandma?" Olivia asked
when Grandma was finished reading.
"This," said Grandma.
"Telling that story?"
"No, being with you!" replied Grandma. "Good night, Olivia."
"Good night, Grandma."